THE
SECRET STARS

BY JOSEPH SLATE · ILLUSTRATED BY FELIPE DAVALOS

MARSHALL CAVENDISH · NEW YORK

Marshall Cavendish, 99 White Plains Road, Tarrytown, New York 10591
The text of this book is set in 20 point Giovanni Bold Condensed
The illustrations are rendered in acrylics.
Printed in Italy
6 5 4 3 2 1

Library of Congress Cataloging-in-Publication Data
Slate, Joseph. The secret stars / written by Joseph Slate ; illustrated by
Felipe Dávalos. — 1st ed.   p.   cm.
Summary: In New Mexico on a rainy, icy Night of the Three Kings,
Sila and Pepe worry that the kings will not be able to use the stars to
navigate, so their grandmother takes them on a magical journey to see
the secret stars all around them.
ISBN 0-7614-5027-0 [1. Stars—Fiction. 2. Epiphany—Fiction.
3. Grandmothers—Fiction. 4. Hispanic Americans—Fiction. 5. New
Mexico—Fiction.] I. Dávalos, Felipe, ill. II. Title.
PZ7.S6289Sf 1998 [E]—dc21 97-20624 CIP AC

For Bill Reiss,
who made it happen
—J. S.

To the light of the stars
—F. D.

It is the night of the Three Kings.
There are no stars in the New Mexico sky.
Rain pelts the pines on Lone Hill.

Suddenly, the rain turns to ice.
It slices down past the pines,
down, down to a little rancho
in the cove of the hill.
It drums the tin roof of the ranch house.
Rat-a-tat-tat, rat-a-tat-tat.

Under the roof, an old grandmother sleeps.
She is the warm hearth on this cold night.
She is the nestling log.
On each side of her a grandchild burrows.
They burrow like kittens.

Rat-a-tat-tat, rat-a-tat-tat.
The star-burst quilt stirs.
The boy Pepe wakes.
Rat-a-tat-tat, rat-a-tat-tat.
The girl Sila wakes.

"Grandma," says Pepe, "how can the Three Kings
ride in such a hard rain?"
"They are strong, they are wise,"
says the grandmother.
"But there will be no stars
to show them the way," says Sila.
"Yes," says Pepe, "how will the Three Kings
find our Baby Manger? How will they find
the hay box for their horses?"
"And the figs?" says Sila.

"And will they bring toys?"
says the grandmother.
She hugs Sila and Pepe.
"I bet someone—I will not mention who—
but I bet someone is wondering,
'Will the Three Kings bring toys?'"

"Maybe just a little *piñata*," says Pepe.
"With toys inside," says Sila.
"And maybe something in our shoes," adds Pepe.
"Maybe," says the grandmother.
"The Three Kings will find a way.
Even if there are clouds.
There are stars behind clouds
and in many secret places."
"What secret places?" asks Pepe.
"Tell us, Grandma, what places?"
The children snuggle close.
They want to hear a story.
A story will shut out the drum-drumming
of the rain.

"Tomorrow, I will show you,"
says the grandmother.
"Tonight, we must sleep,
or the Three Kings will never come."
She rocks Pepe and Sila.
"Let us dream together," she says.
She is like a big bird.
The great quilt is her wings.

Pepe and Sila float in her wings.
"Sail away, sail away," she whispers.
They float and float.
The grandmother and the grandchildren
float.

They circle the room.
They swoop down the stairs.
They hover before the Three Kings on the mantle.
Then they duck under, into the hearth.
Up the chimney they fly.

Outside, the ice storm is over.
The earth sparkles with moonlight.
The air is cold, cold,
but Pepe and Sila are warm.
They are rolled in the wings
of their grandmother's quilt.

The garden lies wasted.
It is under a mantle of ice.
Reeds sparkle and bend.
Two frostflowers twinkle and chime.
"They are secret stars,"
says the grandmother.

A tiny pear-shaped nest is held
by a garden spider's web.
Each strand is laced with ice.
The icy nest glistens.
"Like a star," says Sila.
"And inside," whispers the grandmother,
"each baby is also a star."

They glide over the ranch pond.
Moonlight traces a thin spidery ice
on the cold, clear water.
Deep down, a gold carp shimmers.
Deeper still, in the ooze,
a beaded frog stirs.

"Now," says the grandmother,
"let us see if stars shine
in the chicken coop."

Pepe and Sila laugh.
"Oh Grandma!" says Sila.
"Not in a chicken coop!" says Pepe.
They turn their faces
under their grandmother's arms.
They laugh and wiggle,
tickling their grandmother,
and she laughs too.

In the barred coop, the rooster Reyo
rises to their laughter.
He cranes his stippled neck
across the lines of moonlight.
He will not wake his hens
this cold, cold night.
They roost like puffed white ghosts.

"See Reyo's feathers," whispers the grandmother.
"They spin like stars."
"The hens are the Milky Way,"
says Pepe.
"Oh yes, yes," says Sila.
"I bet they are dreaming."
"Hens dreaming?" says Pepe. "Of what?"
"Of popcorn spilled in the sky,"
says Sila. She claps her hands.

"Shhhhhh," hushes the grandmother.
"There are deer at the barn.
They smell the hay."
The deer raise their horns
to the barn's vented window.
The horns glitter with frost.
"Like stars," says Pepe.

"Now," says the grandmother,
"up, up to the barn windows."
Sila and Pepe break icicles
to see inside the barn.
"Hiya, hiya,"
Pepe calls to the mule Plácido.

Old Plácido looks up.
He nods and stamps.
His eyes run starry tears that glisten.
A halo steams round his head.
"The Three Kings are coming,"
says the grandmother. "Old Plácido knows.
So we must hurry, hurry."

The ranch house is still.
Only a faint light burns
somewhere deep inside it.
Star-frost spatters the window glass.

The three swoop down the chimney.

They duck under the hearth.

Up, up! Their toes skim the stairs.

They flip over.
They hover in the air.
Slowly, they drift down like feathers.

Soon, it is morning.
Pepe and Sila wake.
Their grandmother sleeps.
Tiny blue and red veins thread her cheeks.
"They crisscross like stars," says Pepe.
"Teensy stars," says Sila.

But it is the day of the Three Kings!
They jump out of bed.
They race downstairs.
They lean and push at the front door.
The door yields with a sharp crack.

They lift the lid of the hay box.
The hay is gone. The figs are gone.
There is a painted doll for Sila.
There is a beaded belt for Pepe.
There is a star *piñata*.
There is candy in their shoes.

Pepe and Sila look up at the dawning sky.
"Thank you, thank you, Three Kings,"
they murmur.

High up on Lone Hill,
the pines bend under the ice.
Shadows flicker across their glittering fans.
"Look-ee, look-ee there, Sila," cries Pepe.
"The pines have become the Three Kings!"
"And their crowns and capes," says Sila,
"they are filled with stars."